For Andrew and Peter—S. K.

For the dedicated staff and volunteers at Mission: Wolf—B. S.

SIMON & SCHUSTER BOOKS FOR YOUNG READERS

An imprint of Simon & Schuster Children's Publishing Division

1230 Avenue of the Americas, New York, New York 10020

Text copyright © 2007 by Stephen Krensky

Illustrations copyright © 2007 by Brad Sneed

SIMON & SCHUSTER BOOKS FOR YOUNG READERS is a trademark of Simon & Schuster, Inc.

Book design by Daniel Roode

The text for this book is set in Fontoon.

The illustrations for this book are rendered in watercolor.

Manufactured in China

10 9 8 7 6 5 4 3 2

Library of Congress Cataloging-in-Publication Data

Krensky, Stephen.

Big bad wolves at school / Stephen Krensky; illustrated by Brad Sneed.—1st ed.

p. cm.

Summary: Rufus, a young wolf, has a hard time fitting in at the Big Bad Wolf Academy, where he has been sent to learn to huff and puff, until the day he uses his true talent.

ISBN-13: 978-0-689-83799-9

ISBN-10: 0-689-83799-2

[1. Wolves—Fiction. 2. Identity—Fiction.] I. Sneed, Brad, ill. II. Title.

PZ7.K883Big 2007

[E]—dc22

2005020698

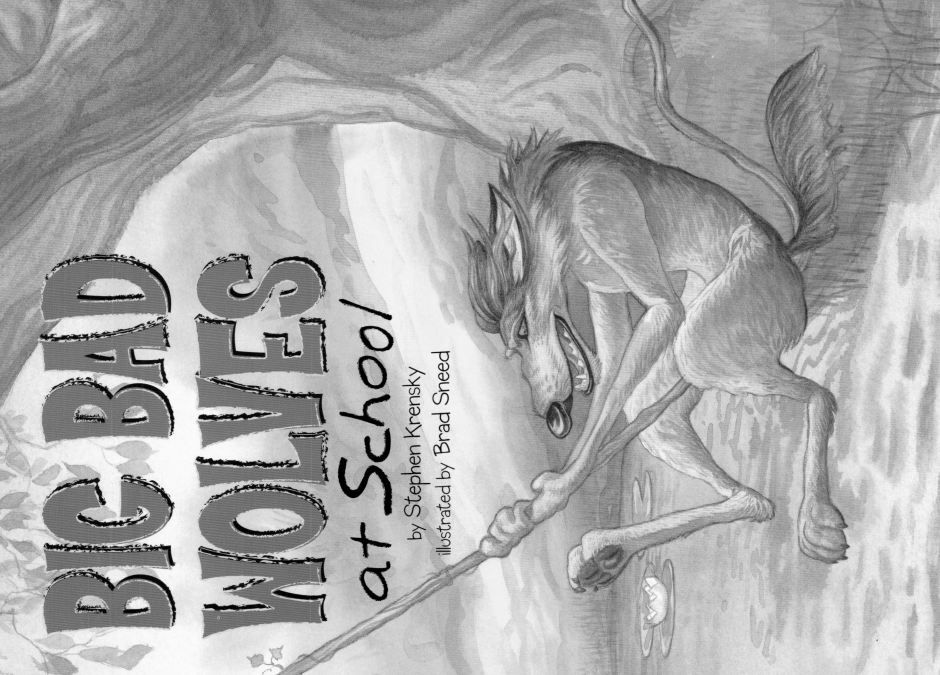

BIG BAD WOLVES
at School

by Stephen Krensky

illustrated by Brad Sneed

SIMON & SCHUSTER BOOKS FOR YOUNG READERS
New York   London   Toronto   Sydney

Rufus was a young wolf who spent his days turning over rocks, rolling in the grass, and running like the wind.

At night he liked to howl at the moon.

Although Rufus seemed happy, his parents were worried.

"Rufus will never survive in the cold, cruel world," said his father.

His mother agreed. "We have to step in before it's too late."

There was only one thing to do.

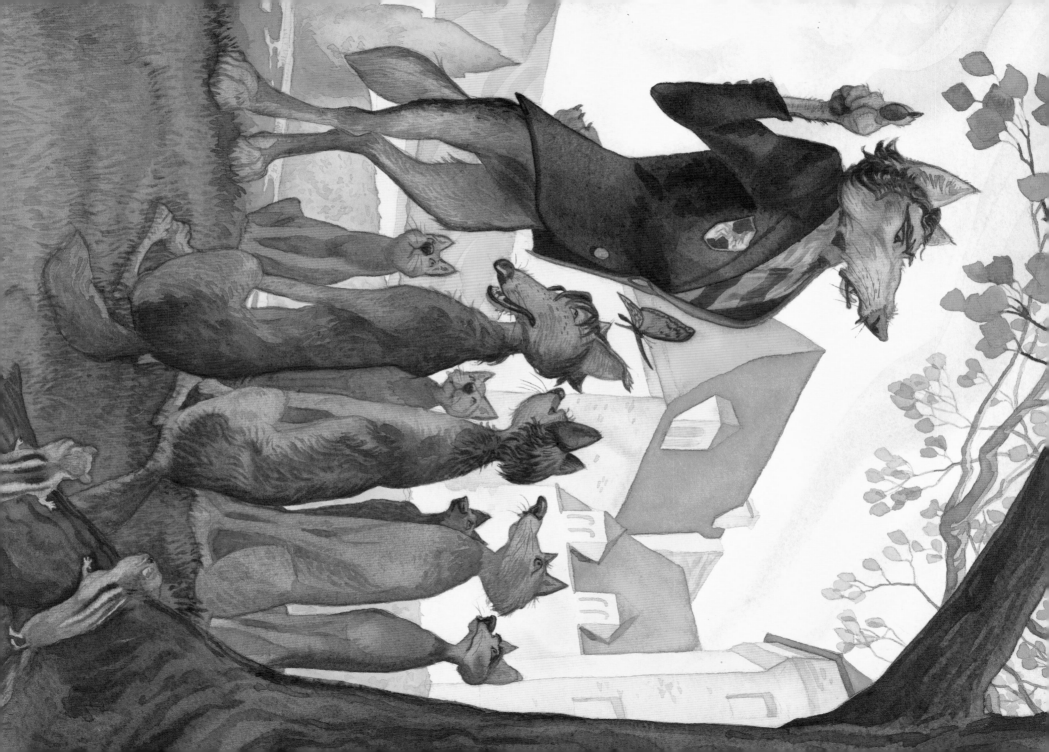

They sent Rufus to the Big Bad Wolf Academy—the toughest school around.

"Straighten up, there!" barked the headmaster, addressing the new arrivals. "You arrive here as ordinary, everyday wolves. But that will change. With hard work and dedication, you will leave as big bad wolves." Most of the new students were impressed.

But not Rufus.

The training began in gym class. There the wolves learned to huff and puff.

"In through the nose!" shouted their instructor. "And out through the mouth!"

Soon, some of the students could blow up a real storm.

But not Rufus.

In acting class the wolves practiced wearing disguises.

"Always put your tail through first," they were told. "That way it won't get squished."

Many of the students were quick learners.

But not Rufus.

Twice a week the students met with the foreign language teacher.

"Say, *Baaaaaa!*" he snapped. "Show some feeling."

"*Baaaaaa!*" the class recited, huddling together.

But not Rufus.

The truth was, Rufus missed his old life. Sometimes he asked the other wolves to go for a run or a swim.

But nobody was interested. "You're so old-fashioned, Rufus," they sniffed, "sticking your nose into everything."

On restless nights Rufus went outside to stretch his legs. He would run back and forth, howling at the moon overhead.

"What pack is that?" the other wolves always shouted out the windows.

"Keep it down! We're trying to sleep."

After a few months the students went on a field trip.

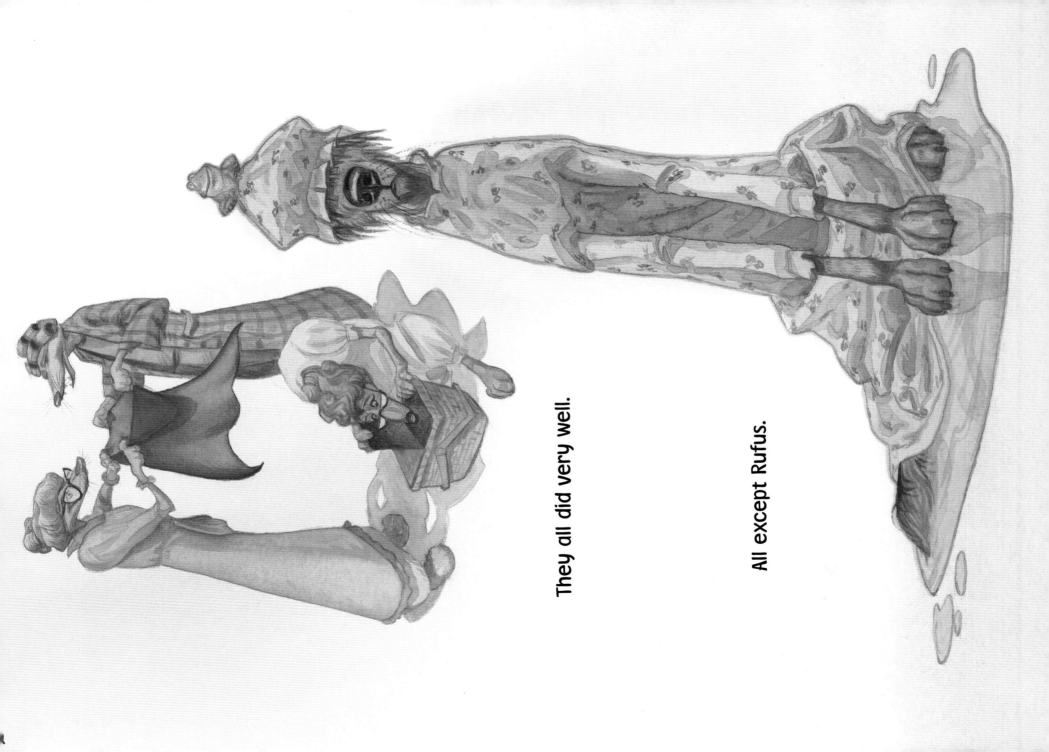

They all did very well.

All except Rufus.

As the seasons passed, the other wolves kept on practicing.

And Rufus felt more and more out of place.

At the end of the year everyone began preparing for final exams.

They studied very hard.

"What's the difference between lurking and sneaking around?"

"Which is easier to wear—a nightgown or pajamas?"

"Is it better to enter a henhouse through the door or a window?"

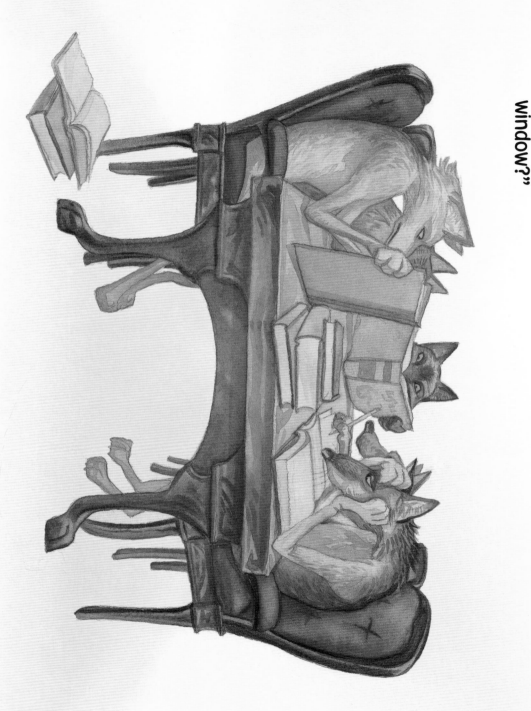

Rufus knew he should be studying too.

But when the sun was shining and the air was clear, there were so many better things to do.

On the first day of testing, Rufus was completely unprepared.

Suddenly, the alarm sounded.

R-R-R-RIINNNG!

"Hunters!" shouted the teacher.

"Prepare to defend yourselves!"

Some of the wolves rushed outside
to huff and puff.

But it did no good.
The hunters held on tight until the
wolves were exhausted.

Others tried to escape in disguise.
That didn't work either.

Rufus was so scared he let out a howl.

Whoooo!

The other wolves stopped to listen.
Many of them had not howled in a long time.
But they were just as scared as Rufus.
One by one, they joined in.
WHHOOOOO! WHHOOOOOO! WHHOOOOOO!

The hunters froze in their tracks and covered their ears.

When Rufus saw what was happening, he got an idea.

Quickly he told the other wolves his plan.

Howling and running, running and howling, the wolves darted through the woods.

WHHOOOOOOOOOOOOOO!

The hunters hesitated.

There were far more wolves than they had ever imagined.

WHHOOOOO! WHHOOOOO! WHHOOOOO! WHHOOOOOO!

The wolves seemed to be everywhere.

"Run for your lives!" the hunters cried, retreating toward the village.

The wolves thanked Rufus for saving them. "You've made us all proud," said the headmaster, handing him a special medal at graduation.

Afterward Rufus and his new friends put away their lessons and returned to the woods.

They ran and wrestled and swam in the lake.

Once a year, though, they returned to a village.

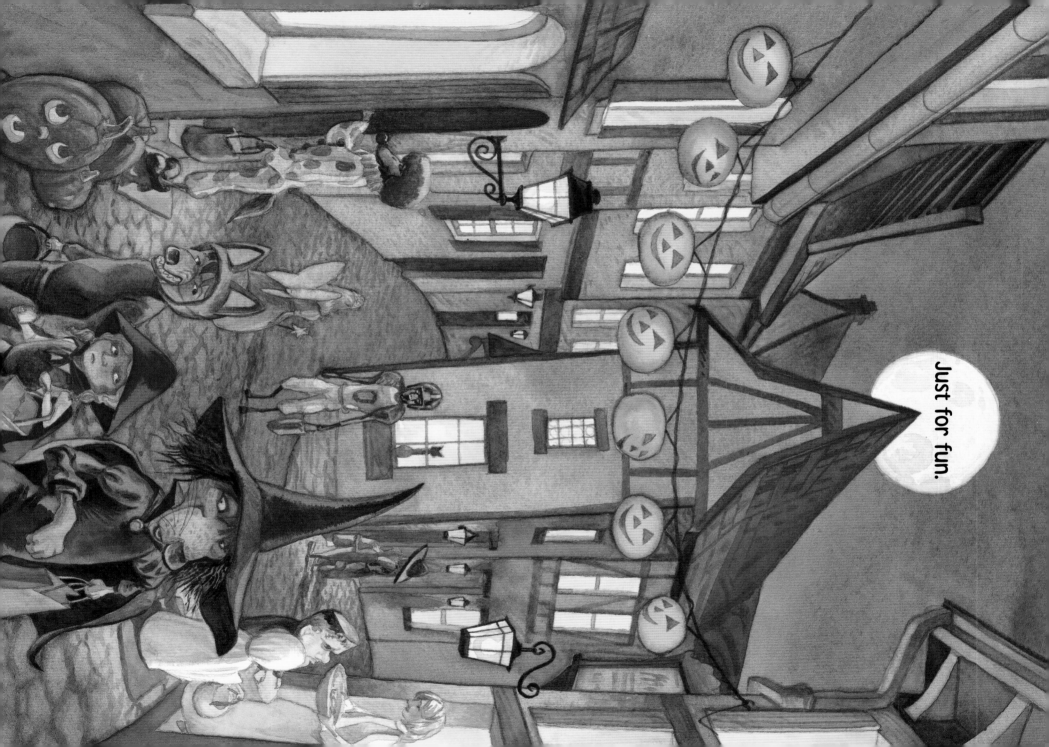

Just for fun.